This book belongs to

_____

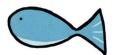

For my children.
You inspire me every day.

First published in 2023 by Pockerley Press
Text copyright © Samantha Cooke
Illustrations copyright © Samantha Cooke

All rights reserved.

No part of this publication may be reproduced, or transmitted in any form, or by any means (electrical, mechanical, photocopying, recording or otherwise) without the written permission of the publishers.

ISBN 978-1-7393414-0-4

Crabby and Seagull

written and illustrated by Samantha Cooke

Far away in another land, a little crab plays in the sand.

But all of a sudden, a crashing wave washes little Crabby away!

He tries,
and tries,
and tries
some more
to get back
to the sandy
shore.

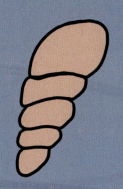

Seagull swoops –
"Come grab my foot!"

But Crabby's arms aren't long enough!

The ocean waves push Crabby down.

He tumbles and twirls and swirls around.

Oh no! Poor Crabby is miles from home!

Will he end up all alone?

Seagull swoops and tries to save,
as Crabby bobs up in a wave.

The BASHING, CRASHING, ocean arms have Crabby in a grip too strong!

Now he's feeling very glum.

Crabby cries "I want my mum!"

A silver flash. A spiky fin.
For Crabby, things look very grim!

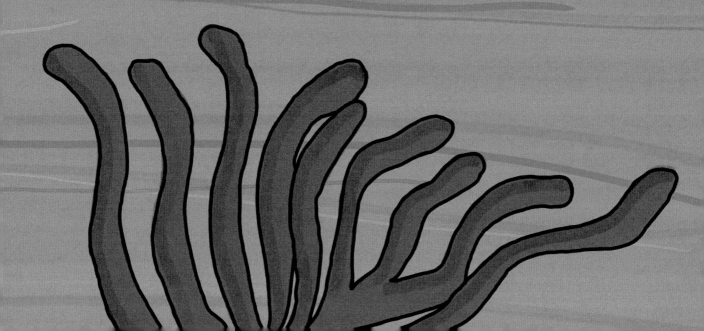

Seagull panics and shouts for help.

That's when he sees the floating kelp.

Down he dives to pick it up.

He clamps his beak and then...

he PULLS!

He pulls so hard his face turns red.

Then up it POPS -

a mermaids head!

"Please help this crab. Oh dear! Oh dear! He was washed away and a shark is near!

I've tried and tried to get him free but his arms are short and my arms are wings!"

"Don't worry Seagull. Do not despair! Crabby, here! Climb up my hair!"

At last, he made it back on land –
his tiny footprints in the sand.

Mermaid smiled and waved goodbye.

Seagull landed by his side.

There they rested by the rocks – both of them were still in shock!

Made in the USA
Middletown, DE
01 April 2025